~The Monkey Tale 1

Stacy, Teal and the Dis_____t

Written by Bunny DiDio Plaske ~ Illustrated by Becky Capps

aBM

Stacy, Teal and the Disappearing Rabbit

Published by:
A Book's Mind
PO Box 272847
Fort Collins, CO 80527
www.abooksmind.com

ISBN 978-1-939828-72-9

Printed in the United States of America

Acknowledgements

To God, for His abundant blessings and the ability
He has provided me to write this book.

To my parents, for providing me a happy childhood and
loving me unconditionally.

To my husband Rich, for believing in me.

To my daughters, Stacy and Teal, you delighted me as children
and continue to bring me infinite joy each and every day.

To my sister Mary, for always being there with an open heart.

To my son-in-law Jim, for the amazing husband and father he is.

To my grandchildren, Emma and Luke, you add a new
dimension of love to my life.

To my friend Carol, for sparking my interest in writing again
and providing me insight and tips.

To my friend Chris, for her unwavering encouragement and support.

To Abba's Writer's Group, for their suggestions and editing.

To Jenene, who transported this book from a dream to a reality.

To Becky, for bringing my words to life.

To the many extended family members and friends who
have taken this journey with me, I am forever grateful.

The Disappearing Rabbit is dedicated to
my daughters, Stacy and Teal.

It's Easter morning, Stacy and Teal's favorite day of the year!

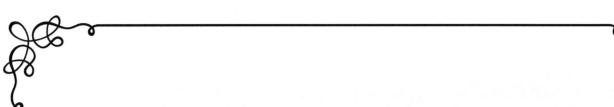

Last night they left a bowl of plastic Easter eggs
for the Easter Bunny to hide.

While they were sleeping, he came and hid them.

"It's so much fun waking up and hunting for eggs," exclaims Teal.

"Let's see who can find the most," says Stacy.

3

Some eggs are easy to find, but a few are hard to spot.

After finding all the eggs, they begin their search for the Easter Basket.
They spy it at the same time hidden behind Daddy's big grey easy chair.

It's filled with jelly beans, peanut butter eggs and pink,
purple and yellow marshmallow chicks.

Their favorite treat of all is the big chocolate rabbit.
Teal and Stacy love chocolate.

It's Daddy's favorite too!

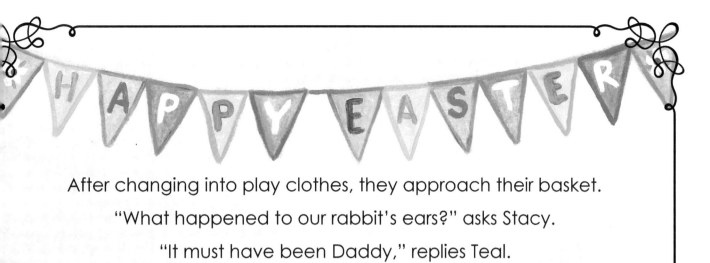

After changing into play clothes, they approach their basket.

"What happened to our rabbit's ears?" asks Stacy.

"It must have been Daddy," replies Teal.

"You know how much he loves chocolate."

"We still have the head, two paws, a belly, two feet and the tail left to eat."

8

Just then, Daddy enters the room.

"Who wants to go for a bike ride?"

"We do!" they shout.

Soon after returning home, they notice the rabbit's head is gone.

"Oh no!" cries Teal. "I think Daddy ate more of our rabbit."

"Don't worry," says Stacy.

"We still have two paws, a belly,
two feet and the tail left to eat.
You know how much
Daddy loves chocolate."

11

Before getting dressed for Easter dinner, they are
taking a bath and spot their basket. "Not again!" yells Teal.
"Our rabbit's paws are gone!"

"It's okay," whispers Stacy.
"You know how much Daddy loves chocolate."

"We still have the belly, two feet and the tail left to eat."

They put on their Easter dress and get ready for dinner.
They peek at their basket.

"I can't believe it!" shouts Stacy.
"Now our rabbit's belly is gone too!"

"It's alright," says Teal.
"You know how much Daddy loves chocolate."

"We still have two feet and the tail left to eat."

After dinner, they make a dash for their basket.

"Our rabbit's two feet are gone! All that's left is his tail!" yells Teal.

"Oh well," replies Stacy.
"You know how much Daddy loves chocolate."

They share the rabbit's tail.

"Yum, that was so delicious," they shout.

"The Easter Bunny will bring us another chocolate rabbit next year," Teal says sadly.

Just then, Mommy enters the room carrying a purple bag.

"I think I ate too much of your chocolate rabbit today."

"It was MOMMY who ate our rabbit!" they screech. Reaching into the bag, Mommy pulls out two big chocolate rabbits!

"These are for my two special girls!"

Stacy and Teal are so excited!
They run to Mommy and wrap their arms around her.

"This is the best Easter ever!"

Bunny Plaske has two grown daughters and two grandchildren. She is a native of Albany, New York and currently resides in Phoenix, Arizona with her husband. Bunny has mentored young children for over twenty-five years including operating a home preschool program. She came to realize, early on, the types of books which held children's interest-ones they wanted to hear again and again.

Bunny would like to take this opportunity to encourage adults to spend quality time with children. Reading and sharing thoughts with a child can create a loving and lasting bond that is priceless.

Becky Capps is a native of Phoenix, Arizona where she has been happily painting murals, canvases and furniture for decades. Illustrating books is her latest endeavor and she will be adding a greeting card line to her repertoire in 2014. She has three grown children and five grandchildren, all who bring her immense joy. You may reach her through her web site www.artisticjoys.com and also see more of her art.

a Book's Mind

Whether you want to purchase bulk copies of
Stacy, Teal and the Disappearing Rabbit
or buy another book for a friend, get it now at:
www.abooksmart.com

If you have a book that you would like to publish,
contact Jenene Scott, Publisher, at A Book's Mind:
jenene@abooksmind.com.

CPSIA information can be obtained
at www.ICGtesting.com
Printed in the USA
BVIC01n1216040414
349706BV00001B/1